PIPER MORGAN
PLANS A PARTY

DON'T MISS ANY OF PIPER'S ADVENTURES!

Piper Morgan Joins the Circus

Piper Morgan in Charge!

Piper Morgan to the Rescue

Piper Morgan Makes a Splash

ALSO BY STEPHANIE FARIS:

30 Days of No Gossip

25 Roses

Best. Night. Ever. *(with six coauthors)*

PIPER MORGAN

PLANS A PARTY

BY STEPHANIE FARIS

ILLUSTRATED BY LUCY FLEMING

♡

ALADDIN

New York London Toronto Sydney New Delhi

ALADDIN

An imprint of Simon & Schuster Children's Publishing Division
1230 Avenue of the Americas, New York, New York 10020
First Aladdin paperback edition November 2017
Text copyright © 2017 by Stephanie Faris
Illustrations copyright © 2017 by Lucy Fleming
Also available in an Aladdin hardcover edition.

For information about special discounts for bulk purchases, please contact Simon & Schuster Special Sales at 1-866-506-1949 or business@simonandschuster.com.
The Simon & Schuster Speakers Bureau can bring authors to your live event. For more information or to book an event contact the Simon & Schuster Speakers Bureau at 1-866-248-3049 or visit our website at www.simonspeakers.com.
Book designed by Laura Lyn DiSiena
The text of this book was set in New Baskerville.
Manufactured in the United States of America 1017 OFF
2 4 6 8 10 9 7 5 3 1
Library of Congress Control Number 2017940876
ISBN 978-1-5344-0386-4 (hc)
ISBN 978-1-5344-0385-7 (pbk)
ISBN 978-1-5344-0387-1 (eBook)

For Jennifer, the best little sister
a girl could have

CHAPTER ★ 1 ★

We were in the middle of nowhere.
In the middle of the middle of nowhere.
We were so far away from "anywhere" that
my mom's cell phone didn't even work.

"Are we lost?" I asked Mom as she
slowed the car and looked down a street
we were about to pass.

"What do the directions say?" Mom
asked.

Oh yeah. Directions. There was this

sheet that had a list of weird things like "1.5 miles turn right on Montvale Lane." I didn't understand what that meant, but I just read them to Mom when she asked.

We were on our way to a ranch. A middle-of-nowhere ranch. There would be real horses, and Mom said I could maybe ride them later if I was really good. It was up to my mom's new client, who had asked us to this ranch. We hadn't met her yet. Just talked to her on the phone.

The ranch is my mom's new job. Well, sort of. My mom's a temp worker, which means she does temporary jobs in lots of different places. This time her job is as an event planner. The event is a birthday party for a girl who lived on a ranch at this place in the mountains. Mom says the people having the party are what you call "loaded." I think that means "really rich."

The hard black road turned into a dirt road when we got closer. Then there was a super-long fence, and that's when I saw them.

"Horses!" I shrieked.

"Piper," Mom said, making a funny face. "Pipe down."

I don't know what that saying means, except "be quiet" for people named Piper. Because it's similar to my name, you see.

I tried to turn all the way around in my seat to see the horses, but it was hard in the booster seat I had to sit on. That was okay, though, because there were more horses there. And there. And *there*.

Horses everywhere!

I was so busy looking at the horses, I almost missed the big, ginormous house up ahead. It was the biggest house I'd ever seen. It was probably even bigger than the school I used to go to before we started moving around. I wondered what it would be like to live in a house that huge.

"The little girl's name is Emmy," Mom said. "She's just a little older than you."

"She's going to be nine!" I guessed. Because I'm seven years old. I kind of wished she was younger than me, because sometimes that meant I got to be boss, which was really awesome. It hadn't happened for a long, long time, though.

I got to carry Mom's folder on the way to the door. I had to hold it carefully so that it wouldn't bend. There were important papers in there that she had gotten from her new boss. Her new client was named Amie with an "ie." I saw her name on Mom's folder full of party-planning ideas.

Mom rang a doorbell, but I didn't hear anything through that huge wooden door. There were windows on either side, but you couldn't see through the glass because it was so pretty and colorful, like glass in a church.

After the longest wait ever, the door opened. The fanciest woman I'd seen in my entire life was standing there, holding a small puppy. It looked almost as cute as my nanna's dog, Oreo.

"Yes?" the woman asked, looking over the top of my mom's head.

"Julie Morgan," my mom said. "My boss sent me over to get information about your event."

"Of course," she said. "Come in."

I followed Mom inside the house, staring up at the tall ceilings. There was one of those big chandelier things hanging above us. The floor was marble and there were pretty marble stairs on both sides of the room. I felt like I was in a celebrity's house or something.

"Are you a star?" I asked the woman with the dog.

It was a good question, I thought. Mom hadn't told me who this woman was, just that she had a daughter. Celebrities could have kids too, I was pretty sure.

"Excuse me?" the woman asked.

She looked at me for the first time. I wondered if she'd even noticed me there. I was pretty short.

"Maybe Piper would like to play with Emmy," Mom suggested.

"Of course," the woman said, pointing to the backyard. "She's out there . . . somewhere."

I waited for someone to take me, but nobody did. Mom gave me a look that said, *Go on*, so that's exactly what I did. I walked out the back doors and that's where I found Emmy.

Confetti Fact #1

Birthday parties as we know them today started in the 1700s in Germany. Kids got a cake and one candle for each year, plus one "to grow on." Grown-ups told the kids to make a wish and blow out the candles—something we still do today.

Some think putting candles on a cake actually started in ancient Greece. The Greeks made a round cake, topped it with lit candles, and offered it to Artemis, the moon goddess. Legend says that the smoke from the candles took the wishes of anyone offering the cake to the gods in the sky.

CHAPTER

★ 2 ★

Emmy was talking to her tablet.

Only when I got closer did I see there was a face on that tablet. I couldn't see much, though. It was too sunny out there and she was sitting in a lounge chair.

"My mom's meeting with the stupid party planner about my stupid party," Emmy was saying to the screen. "It's all just—"

"You're not supposed to say 'stupid.'" I

interrupted before she could say it again. "It's not a nice word."

Emmy didn't look surprised to see me back there at all. I could see her eyeballs as she looked at me over the top of her sunglasses. Wait. Maybe I shouldn't start off like this.

"I'm Piper Morgan," I said proudly.

"So?" Emmy asked.

"Emmy!" the girl on the screen said. "Be nice."

"She's just the party planner's kid," Emmy said, saying the word "kid" like she wasn't one. "I don't have to be nice to her."

"You should be nice to everyone," I said.

There I went again. This wasn't how you made friends.

"Hi," I said, waving to the girl in the tablet. Emmy had turned the screen and I could kind of see the face better. She had bangs. I didn't know anyone with bangs.

"Hi," the girl said, waving. "I'm Kylie."

"I'm Piper," I said, even though I'd already said that to Emmy.

"I'm having a birthday party too," Kylie said. "It's going to be at the roller-skating rink."

A roller-skating party sounded like more fun than a backyard party. I wondered why Emmy hadn't done one of those.

"Are you going to be at Emmy's party?" Kylie asked.

"I hope," I said. "My mom said it depends."

"The guest list is full," Emmy said, sounding more annoyed than ever. She looked at me with a fake smile. "Sorry."

"I won't be a guest," I said. "I'll be working."

Emmy laughed, but it came out like a snort. "You're too young to work."

"No, I'm not!" I protested. "I've worked in a circus and a principal's office and at a pet-rescue shelter. I was even in a TV commercial for a pool store."

"Good," Emmy said. "Maybe you can fix our pool filter. It's clogged."

"Emmy!" Kylie said.

Emmy sighed. "Gotta go," she said to the face on her screen. "Text me later."

Without waiting for her friend to say good-bye, she pushed a button. And the tablet was just a black screen with no person's picture in it. I wanted a tablet. But mostly I wanted a friend to appear in it. I haven't had a best friend to talk to in a long time.

"My parties are *the best*," Emmy said,

standing and turning to face me. "The best. Your mom hasn't thrown a birthday party like mine before."

She was right about that. But my mom had the best birthday parties for me. She always got the cake I liked, and we always did something fun with my friends.

"I'm going to help," I said with a big smile.

"No," Emmy said. "Just no! Only your mom."

The smile went from my face. *Poof*, it was gone. I wanted to help. I wanted to help so, so much.

"I can make sure you get everything you want," I said quickly, before she could say more. "You tell me and I'll help."

Her eyes narrowed as she looked at me. She was thinking about it. I could tell she was really, really thinking about it. Finally, she picked up her tablet and clutched it to her chest.

"Come on," Emmy said. "Let's plan a party."

Confetti Fact #2

If you've ever been to a birthday party, you've probably heard a song called "Happy Birthday to You." It's a song everyone knows, no matter how old they are. Here are a few fun facts about the birthday song.

#1 TWO TEACHERS WROTE THE SONG IN 1893. THEY WERE ALSO SISTERS.

#2 UNTIL RECENTLY NOBODY COULD SING "HAPPY BIRTHDAY TO YOU" IN A MOVIE WITHOUT PAYING LOTS OF MONEY. BUT THERE WAS A LAWSUIT AND NOW MOVIES CAN USE IT FOR FREE.

#3 "HAPPY BIRTHDAY TO YOU" IS ONE OF THE MOST SUNG ENGLISH SONGS IN THE WORLD.

CHAPTER
★ 3 ★

"No clowns!"

That was the first thing Emmy blurted when we sat down at their fancy, huge kitchen table to talk about the party. My mom actually wrote the words "No clowns" on her notepad.

"Emmy is a bit afraid of clowns," Emmy's mom said with a big smile.

"Am not!" Emmy shrieked. "I don't like them."

"Okay, Emmy," her mom said. "Let's be nice."

Could Emmy be nice? I didn't think so. But her face wasn't as scrunchy when she looked at us.

"And jelly beans," she said. "Those are my favorite."

Mom added jelly beans to the list.

"Preferably pink," Amie told my mom. "She really only likes the pink ones."

"Only pink *everything*," Emmy said. "You can have some white, but no other colors."

My mom didn't write that down right away. I thought that

might mean she'd say no. She didn't.

"And I want princesses," Emmy said. "Not fake princesses, but *real* ones."

"Princesses aren't real," I said with a laugh.

"Of course they are," Emmy said back. She wasn't making a nice face. It was all scrunched up again, like it had been before her mother told her to be nice.

"You're right, Emmy. Princesses *are* real," Emmy's mom said, smiling at her. "And we're going to have real ones at this party."

"Of course, sounds great," Mom said, writing "real princesses" on her notepad.

I knew there were real princesses, of course. But real princesses didn't go to birthday parties. They were in other places, living in castles and doing princessy things. I didn't understand how my mother could get real princesses to go to a nine-year-old's birthday party.

"And I want a pink dress," Emmy said. "Not just any dress, but the prettiest pink dress in the whole wide world."

I looked at Mom. Did party planners buy dresses, too? I thought they just planned the party.

"Umm," Mom said. She froze, pen above the paper.

"We'll find one!" I said.

I could tell from my mom's "umm" that this wasn't something party planners were supposed to do. But I didn't want her to get fired. If she got fired, Emmy would be right about me being "just the party planner's kid" and not having to be nice to me.

If we were the best party planners in the history of birthday parties, she'd have to be nice to me.

"I'll handle buying the dress," Emmy's mom said, giving her daughter a look. I could tell Emmy made her mom feel *exasperated* a lot. That's a word I make my mom feel too.

As we headed to our car, Emmy's wish list on Mom's notepad, I asked her about the dress. Not about Emmy's dress. This was much more important than that.

"Can I get a pretty new dress too?" I asked.

"Of course," Mom said. "We have to look our best for the party, even though we'll be working."

"Can it be sparkly?" I asked. Since she was saying yes, may as well ask for everything.

"We'll see," Mom said.

I'd had dresses before in my life, but not too many. Most of the time I just wore jeans or shorts or leggings. I hoped I could get a princesslike dress, to match the real princesses Mom was going to find for the party.

"Thank you for your help with all this," Mom said in the car on the way to the dress place the next morning. "You've been really good with Emmy."

I let out a big sigh. "It isn't easy. She's a handful."

Mom laughed at that. Probably because it wasn't something a seven-year-old would normally say. When you worked around grown-ups, eventually you started to talk like them, that's all.

"I'm going to need you to help me at the party," Mom said. "Emmy may get upset when she sees that we don't have real princesses."

"Yeah, 'cause those would be expensive."

I'd love to meet a real-life princess, but Mom said real princesses didn't go to little girls' birthday parties. That's what I thought she'd say. Plus, most princesses live far, far away, so they'd have to fly a bazillion hours to get here. That just isn't going to happen, Mom said.

"Help her see the good things, not the bad," Mom said.

"Okay, but I think it'll be much easier to do if I'm wearing a sparkly dress," I said.

Mom looked at me quickly, then back at the road. I could see the smile tugging at the corners of her mouth, though. She thought I was funny and that was okay. As long as I got to buy a sparkly dress.

Confetti Fact #3

Have you ever seen the words "Please RSVP" on an invitation?

It basically means, "Please let us know if you're coming."

"RSVP" stands for a French phrase: *"Répondez s'il vous plaît,"* which translates as "Reply if you please." People started using RSVP on invitations in the mid-1800s, but by the early 1900s, experts said it was going out of style. To this day, though, people will include RSVP on invitations to important events like weddings.

CHAPTER
★ 4 ★

We'd had five days to put Emmy's party together. Five days of cupcake tasting and jelly-bean searching and Mom calling every place in town to find a princess who wouldn't wear the typical princess costumes. Something more like a princess you'd see today instead of what you'd see in a fairy tale or movie, she told them.

By Saturday morning I was super tired. More tired than I'd ever been in my whole life. Mom said being a party planner was so, so fun, but very hard work. I'd figured out I agreed with that.

I was running to keep up with my mom when I heard the scream. Mom was carrying a giant punch bowl and all the punch ingredients. We were late, so everything was moving really, really fast.

"Uh-oh," Mom said. "Someone's throwing a fit."

It was probably Emmy. I don't know why I thought that. There were probably a bazillion eight- and nine-year-olds at this birthday party. I just had a feeling it was Emmy.

"No!"

Another scream, this one much closer. Mom's steps slowed a little. I slowed down too. I didn't want to run ahead of her, even though I wanted everyone to see my super-sparkly dress. In the sunlight it was even sparklier than it was in our hotel room.

I finally looked up. I'd been looking down at the napkins I was carrying because I could watch my sparkly dress. When I looked up, I saw where the screams had been coming from: Emmy, who was standing right in front of us.

"No!" she yelled for a third time.

"Hi, Emmy!" Mom called out. "Don't you look pretty."

Emmy didn't answer. She was too busy staring at me. And the look on her face was not a happy one.

"No pink!" she yelled. "You're wearing pink?"

I looked down at my sparkly dress. Yes,

it was pink. It was the sparkliest one of all the dresses I'd seen at the store, and besides, I liked pink. Pink was a fun color for dresses.

"Pink is *my* color!" Emmy said way too loudly. She was yelling like we were far, far away, but now we were close up.

She *was* wearing pink. And everything behind her was pink. I'd helped Mom pick most of it out. It was a pink, pink party.

I probably had pink on the brain. But now I was in trouble.

"I like your dress," I said. Maybe saying something nice would help. "We match!"

Not really, except we were both pink.

"You have to change!" Emmy said. "You have to."

Change? But I liked this dress. Besides, I didn't have anything different to wear.

"Moooom!" Emmy screeched at the top of her voice. It made my ears hurt it was so loud. It worked, though. Emmy's mom came from somewhere behind Emmy. She ran straight toward us.

"What?" she asked. "What's going on? Oh, hi!"

That last part was directed at me and my mom. Emmy's mom's face looked all scrunched, which probably meant she was stressed. My mom got that look sometimes too.

"If you don't mind, I'll just go get started," Mom told Emmy's mom. Which meant she left me there alone. With Emmy and Emmy's mom.

Emmy's mom put her hand on her shoulder. "Emmy, let's go back to the party. Your friends are starting to arrive."

"No!" Emmy said again. And this time she added a foot stomp to her shout. "I'm not going back until *she* changes."

And with that, Emmy spun around and ran toward the house. Her pink, not-sparkly dress blew out as she ran, making it even prettier. Maybe I should have picked a not-sparkly dress.

"Maybe you could wear a different dress?" Emmy's mom asked. "I know she's being . . . unreasonable, but I just want this party to go well." She rubbed her eyes and leaned against a big table that had two pictures of Emmy on it, one as a baby and one now. There was a pretty sign with Emmy's name spelled out, and there were some of what I figured were Emmy's favorite things—some stuffed animals, a sparkly bow, a pair of ballet shoes.

"I don't have another dress," I said. I mean, that *should* be obvious, right? Why would I carry an extra dress around with me?

"Emmy probably has something you can wear," her mom said. "Let's go find her."

Confetti Fact #4

Pink is a very popular color. But if you don't call it your favorite, you aren't alone. Blue is actually the most popular color in the world. But there are some fun facts about pink that make it a pretty cool color.

#1 ALTHOUGH THE COLOR PINK HAS BEEN AROUND FOR CENTURIES, THE WORD "PINK" WASN'T ASSIGNED AS A COLOR NAME UNTIL THE LATE SEVENTEENTH CENTURY.

#2 THE NAME CAME FROM FLOWERS CALLED "PINKS."

#3 ONE STORY SAYS THAT GIRLS WERE BORN INSIDE PINK ROSES. EVEN TODAY IT'S STILL TRADITION FOR BABY GIRLS TO BE DRESSED IN PINK.

CHAPTER
★ 5 ★

When we got to Emmy's bedroom, the door was locked.

"Emmy!" her mom said after knocking a bazillion times. "Open this door now!"

"No!"

She was still yelling that word. That was all she was yelling.

"What's going on?"

That was Kylie. She must have heard the commotion and run upstairs. She was standing there with a frowny face. And she had on a pink dress too!

"Hi, Kylie. She's mad that I have a pink dress on," I said.

"Oh!" Kylie said.

She nodded like she knew what that meant. Emmy hadn't seen Kylie yet. Emmy was going to be *really* mad to see that two of us were in pink.

"And now she won't come out," I added.

"Let me try," Kylie offered.

Emmy's mom stepped aside, and Kylie walked up to the door.

"Emmy?" she asked. "It's Kylie. Can I come in?"

Silence. We waited for lots and lots of seconds for the door to unlock or for Emmy to say something. She said nothing.

There was a party going outside. My

mom had worked super hard to make it the best birthday party ever. And now Emmy was ruining it. I couldn't let that happen.

"I'll change my dress," I called out. "I just need another dress to wear. You can pick."

We waited. After a while Emmy's mom sighed.

"I need to go check and see if more people are here. Let me know if you girls need anything." With that, she turned and walked downstairs. I wondered if maybe Kylie and I should go enjoy the party too, even if it was without the birthday girl!

But then we heard a *click*. The door opened just a crack. I saw one of Emmy's eyeballs and a strip of her face.

"Only Kylie and Piper," Emmy said.

That made me feel special. Like I was

her friend too, even though I knew that wasn't true.

"Don't worry, it's just me and Piper," Kylie said.

Emmy opened the door to let us in. As soon as we were inside, she slammed the door and locked it.

"I'll pick something out for you," Emmy said to me. She marched to her closet.

I looked at Kylie, who shrugged her pink-dress-covered shoulders. I wanted to ask why I had to change and Kylie didn't, but that would make Emmy mad.

While I waited for Emmy to come out with a dress, Kylie went to the window to look out at the party. After a few minutes she gasped.

"What?" I asked.

I didn't wait for her to answer. I rushed

over to the window to see what she was seeing.

The first thing I noticed was the crowd. They formed a wide circle around two kids who were pulling on something. At first it looked like they were playing tug-of-war, but then I realized they were tugging on some kind of stuffed animal, one that I had seen on the table earlier.

"Bugsy!" Emmy shrieked, causing both Kylie and me to jump. At some point she'd come out of the closet and was standing next to Kylie. "*Here.* I have to get down there."

She tossed something at me and ran. She didn't even close the bedroom door after her, so we were staring into the empty hallway.

I looked down at the dress I was wearing. It wasn't sparkly at all. It was a plain gray color, but the color was the only thing plain. There were bows and puffy sleeves and all kinds of weird designs all over it. It was the ugliest dress I'd ever, ever seen. Ever.

But I knew I had to wear it. We couldn't go on with the party unless I did. If we messed up the party, Emmy would tell all her friends, "See? I was right about Piper. She's no good at throwing parties." I wanted everyone to see that I was the best party thrower in the whole wide world.

"Excuse me," I said, going to the walk-in closet and closing the door. Time to put on the ugliest dress any girl ever wore. Ever.

Confetti Fact #5

Dressing up in a fancy dress can be *so* much fun. Dresses have come a long way over the years, but some things are always the same. Silk and lace and bling have always been popular in party dresses. Here are a few facts you probably didn't know about dresses.

#1 WOMEN ONCE WORE OLD GOLD COINS ON THEIR DRESSES TO ADD SOME BLING. THEY WERE CALLED "SEQUINS."

#2 WEDDING DRESSES HAVEN'T ALWAYS BEEN WHITE. UNTIL THE 1800S PEOPLE THOUGHT A WHITE DRESS WOULD GET DIRTY TOO EASILY. THEY WERE RIGHT ABOUT THAT.

#3 UNTIL THE EARLY 1900S, IT WAS VERY COMMON FOR YOUNG BOYS TO WEAR DRESSES.

CHAPTER
★ 6 ★

All the kids were playing hide-and-go-seek when I came out. I saw Emmy and Kylie and six other girls. I felt left out for a second, but then I remembered. I wasn't part of the party. I was helping Mom.

"Piper!" Mom said as I got closer. "What on earth?"

I knew she was talking about my dress. I could tell her Emmy made me wear it, but she looked super stressed.

"Isn't it nice?" I asked, turning in a circle. "Emmy let me wear it."

"It's certainly . . ." She looked all the way down at the bottom of the skirt part of the dress. It went almost to my ankles. "Different?"

"It is! Nobody has a dress like mine anywhere."

I looked over at the other girls. Aside from Kylie, no pink at all. There was blue and white and even light purple. But no pink.

I thought of something then. Kylie and Emmy were best friends. The kind of best friends that wore the same color together. Of course Emmy wouldn't make Kylie change. Only me.

"Ready?" Emmy yelled. "Set! Go!"

Everyone jumped up and ran in different directions. I wanted to run too, but Mom needed me.

I followed Mom to the car, where she had the rest of the food. We set it all up on the table while I tried not to look at the other kids, who were all hiding behind trees and stuff. Emmy's friend Kylie was hiding under the table. Emmy was running around tagging people.

I was helping my mom with the plastic knives and forks when I heard Emmy crying again. Her cry was loud.

"I want a *real* princess!" she shouted in between sobs.

Mom sighed. I knew that sigh well. She was *exhausted*. "Exhausted" is something that happens when moms get exasperated too much.

"I guess the princess isn't a hit," she said.

I turned around to look at the princess Mom had picked. She was wearing a crown. She looked super pretty, but not like a fairy-tale princess. She could have been a *real* princess. But she wasn't.

"I'll go talk to her," I said to my mom.

I had no idea what I was going to say once I got there. All I wanted to do was make things better.

"It's okay," I said to the princess, who was still smiling even though her eyes looked confused.

I cleared my throat and spoke loudly so that Emmy could hear me over her crying.

"Emmy doesn't know that you're better than a real princess," I said.

Emmy stopped making so much noise. She looked at us. She still looked mad, but she seemed like she'd listen to whatever I'd say next.

"Real princesses don't get to come to parties like this," I said. "They live in palaces over in other countries. This princess gets to pick from all the birthday parties in all the whole world. And she picked Emmy's. That makes her better than a real princess. She's *your* princess, Emmy."

Emmy looked like she wasn't sure whether she should believe me. But she didn't cry. She just nodded and let the princess join the game.

Smiling to myself, I walked back to the cake table. Mom was standing there watching me.

"Wow!" she said. "You handled that really well. I'm proud of you."

I smiled. "I'm proud of you" were my

favorite words. Especially when my mom said them.

"I forgot the cake knife," Mom said. "I'll be right back. Keep an eye on things."

I'd been standing there just a few seconds when I heard Emmy behind me.

"I don't want to wait!" she yelled.

I was staring at the pretty cake. It was white with big pink dots and three cakes stacked on top of one another. The top cake was shaped like a crown.

I turned around to see Emmy's mom looking down at her. She had a frown on her face. It didn't look like things were going well.

"You can play with the princess and eat cake after we eat some other food," Emmy's mom said. "This is the schedule and we're sticking to it."

"But I don't want to!" Emmy screamed. Kids started coming out of hiding. They looked like they didn't know what to do.

"We have food!" I shouted. "Look at your pretty cake."

Emmy looked at me. I held my breath. I knew she would tell me she'd already seen her cake. Or something like that.

But her not-so-happy look changed. She actually smiled.

"I want a piece of cake now," Emmy said. "It's my cake, so I get to choose when I eat it!"

"My mom went to get the cake knife," I told her. But Emmy was standing right in front of the cake now, eyeing it with a big smile on her face.

"I think I want this piece," she said, putting her hand near the bottom of the

cake. There were two layers above it and I was pretty sure they'd fall if she wasn't careful.

"You should wait for my mom," I told her. "She'll be here in just a second."

I looked nervously to my right and saw my mom heading toward us. I thought about telling her to hurry up, but maybe I could talk Emmy out of this. Maybe my mom would never have to find out.

Out of the corner of my eye, I saw Emmy dig her right hand into the bottom layer of the cake and pull out a huge chunk. The top two layers fell downward to fill the big hole that had been left.

The cake was collapsing!

Before I could figure out what to do, my mom got to the table. I was in big, big trouble.

Confetti Fact #6

Hide-and-go-seek has been around for many years. People don't know exactly when it started, but they think it comes from an ancient Greek game called *apodidraskinda*. One person closes his or her eyes and everyone else hides. The person has to find everyone before they get back to home base.

In the game most kids play today, one person finds everyone. The last person found gets to be the finder for the next game.

You can even make up your own version of hide-and-go-seek to play with your own friends. The rules change all the time.

CHAPTER ★ 7 ★

My mom had that look on her face. It was a look I'd seen before when I'd messed up. But I wasn't worried about that. I was too busy worrying that she was about to be fired.

When she worked at the circus and pool shop, I didn't want that to happen. I wanted her to work at those places forever and ever and ever. This time it was okay if we went somewhere else. Emmy was mean,

ing up the handful of cake she'd grabbed
from the bottom.

"That's bad manners,"
I said. "My mom was
going to cut it and give
everyone a nice piece."

"Okay," Mom said

as she approached. "It's okay. We'll fix this. Help me, Piper."

My frown wanted to turn into a big smile, but I kept it from doing that. I still had to look annoyed. But I was so happy to be able to help my mom fix things. She shoved a bunch of napkins into the hole to prop the cake back up, then started carefully cutting slices. I held up each plate for a slice, then set them all out neatly on the table, side by side.

By the time we were finished, girls were lining up for cake. I didn't forget the most important thing, though. I asked Mom for the candles and put nine of them in a big slice of cake. Then Mom carried it over to Emmy while everyone sang the "Happy Birthday" song.

"Hey, Piper!"

Now I knew that voice. It was Kylie.

"My birthday at the roller rink is next weekend," Kylie said. "Can you come?"

I smiled. I'd never been invited to a roller-skating party before. I looked at Mom, who nodded before returning to her cake slicing.

"I might also need your help with a few things," she said. "We have the cake already, but do you think you could help me decorate?"

The best thing about this was that she was asking me, not my mom. I'd still have to get my mom's help—and my mom's boss would make them pay money—but I felt happy anyway. Somebody had asked me to help with something. That was the best thing ever.

Confetti Fact #7

Princesses are in a lot of the fairy tales we read and the movies we see, but there really are princesses in the world. Here are a few fun things to know about real-life princesses.

#1 PRINCESSES WEREN'T EVEN CALLED PRINCESSES UNTIL THE LATE 1300S. UNTIL THEN THEY WERE JUST CALLED "LADY."

#2 TO BECOME A PRINCESS, YOU HAVE TO EITHER HAVE PARENTS WHO ARE PART OF THE ROYAL FAMILY OR MARRY A PRINCE.

#3 OF ALL THE DISNEY PRINCESSES, SNOW WHITE IS THE YOUNGEST. SHE'S SUPPOSED TO BE ONLY FOURTEEN YEARS OLD!

CHAPTER
★ 8 ★

"This is going to be the best birthday party *ever*!"

I said that because I knew it was true. You know why? I helped plan it. My mom helped too. Plus, it was the best place to have a birthday party for a nine-year-old. A roller-skating rink!

I'd never had a party in a roller-skating rink, but I loved to skate, so I knew it would be super fun. Plus, the person I was talking to was Kylie. It was her party. And she looked excited too.

"Let's get our skates!" she said.

"Can we go get our skates?" I asked Mom.

Mom and I had been there for a whole half hour before Kylie got there. We'd unloaded everything from the car and set up the party room so it was ready. When Kylie saw it, she had a huge smile.

"Sure," Mom said. "Go have fun."

Kylie ran toward the skate-rental area and I ran too. I had to keep up. We put our skates on so fast, I barely had time to tie my laces. Then we skated as fast as we could through the snack area to get to the rink.

There wasn't even music, but we didn't care. We had the whole floor to ourselves.

That wouldn't last long, so I knew we had to have fun while we could.

Kylie grabbed my hand and we skated along. We were laughing and smiling and having the best time ever.

Until we saw Emmy.

Kylie saw her first. She slowed down a little and I couldn't figure out why. Then I saw where she was looking. Emmy was standing at the side of the rink with her arms crossed over her chest. She did not look happy.

"Come out and skate!" I called out. Because this was a party and I wanted everyone to have fun.

"No!" Emmy said. Her favorite word.

"Let's go to her," Kylie said.

It was her birthday, so I had to do what she wanted. She let go of my hand and

skated straight to Emmy, who was pouting.

"You should have waited for me," Emmy said. She was looking at Kylie. I was just invisible, I guess.

"Hi, Emmy!" I said.

She didn't even look at me.

"I'm sorry," Kylie said. "We wanted to skate."

All of a sudden the music started. I looked up at the clock and saw it was time for the party. Everyone was late.

"I'll go get my skates," Emmy said.

"I'll go with you," Kylie said.

They rushed off without waiting for me. I wondered if I was supposed to go with them. Emmy didn't seem to want me to. I decided to go look out the window to see if there were people in the parking lot.

"What are you doing, Piper?" Mom

asked, coming over to the window. My face was pressed against it.

"Nobody's out there," I said. "The parking lot is empty."

She looked, then glanced at her phone.

"I'm sure they're all riding together," she said. "Come help me with something."

There wasn't really anything she needed me to do. She just wanted to take my mind off the empty parking lot. We rearranged the place mats and messed with the party hats, and five whole minutes went by. Still no people.

"Can we send them a text?" I asked.

My mom had everyone's mom's number stored in her phone as a group text. It was part of the way she shared information about the party, since people didn't always check their e-mail. She only texted them one or two times so they didn't get mad, she told me.

She checked the window one more time, then looked at Emmy and Kylie, who were skating by themselves. Then she sent a group text. Immediately, she got a text back from one of the moms.

"Emmy told her mom it was moved to the ice rink," Mom said. "The other moms took their kids there."

"Ice rink?" I said. "But Kylie doesn't like ice-skating. She said she doesn't know how."

Mom was thinking hard, though. I knew her thinking-hard face. I'd seen it lots.

"I think Emmy sabotaged the party," Mom said.

Now I had my thinking-hard face on. I knew what "sabotage" meant. It meant Emmy did something to make it not go well. She told everyone to go somewhere else so nobody would show up for Kylie's party.

"I'll get them here," Mom said. "Then we'll deal with Emmy."

We didn't have to deal with Emmy together. I wanted to talk to her. I *would* talk to her.

I skated out to catch up with them.

Confetti Fact #8

Roller-skating has been a favorite American pastime. For hundreds of years people have been putting wheels on their feet and skating around. It wasn't always a big rink where people skated in circles. It actually started in the 1700s, when John Joseph Merlin showed up at a masquerade party wearing wheels on his shoes. He fell in front of everyone.

These days, roller-skating is mostly popular for families and kids. It's a great place to have a birthday party or go for a fun day out. But did you know it's also healthy? Plus, it's more fun than some other types of exercise.

CHAPTER ★ 9 ★

"Emmy!" I called out. I had to call that out because she was still ignoring me.

After skating a few steps, she slowed to a stop and turned to face me. You could do that when you were one of only three skaters on the floor.

"What?" she asked in a not-nice voice.

"We need to talk," I said.

I said that in the same voice my mom

used when I was in trouble. Emmy was in trouble.

"So talk," she said, shifting her weight from one foot to the other.

"Alone," I said. "It'll just take a minute."

I said that last part to Kylie, who shrugged and skated off. She left the floor and went to the party room. I hoped Mom wouldn't say anything about what Emmy had done. It might hurt Kylie's feelings.

"The party has changed places?" I asked.

"What are you talking about?" she asked. But she didn't look at my eyes when she said it. I thought that meant she was nervous about what she was saying.

"I know you told everyone to go to another skating rink," I said. "One of the other moms told my mom. You're sabotaging the party."

I worried for a second that Emmy wouldn't know what "sabotaging" meant. If she didn't, she didn't mention it.

"You can't prove it," she said.

"Everyone's on the way here," I said. "My mom will speak to one of their moms. You could be in big trouble."

For the first time ever, Emmy looked like she might actually not be in charge. I kind of, sort of liked her when she looked like that. With that look on her face, she might be nice to me.

But then I remembered what she'd done to Kylie. That wasn't very nice.

"Okay," she said finally. "You're right."

"You sabotaged the party?" I asked.

"Yes."

Now the important part. "Why?"

She didn't answer for a very long time. It seemed like half a song played before she said something. I looked around nervously, but other kids weren't showing up yet. We still had a little time.

"You took my best friend," she said loudly.

I was so surprised, I didn't know what to say. I thought quickly, trying to figure out what to say next.

"I was just helping Kylie plan the party," I said. "We aren't best friends. *You're* her best friend."

"She talks about you all the time," Emmy said. "She likes you better than me. I just wanted her to see that I'm her best friend, not you."

"By being the only person who showed

up for her birthday party?" I asked. "That would hurt her feelings."

"I know." She looked down at the ground. I could still see her face, though, and she had a sad expression. "I didn't really think about that."

"You have to make it up to her," I said.

She lifted her head. "There's something else," she said. "I haven't been very nice to you."

I was surprised again. Was Emmy actually . . . *apologizing*?

"I didn't want you to take my best friend," she said. "I was mean. I'm sorry."

"Thank you," I said with a smile.

"People are starting to show up," Emmy said, pointing to the door, where a group of kids now gathered. "I'll go apologize to Kylie."

"No!" I said. "Don't. Just help me make this the best birthday party ever. That's all you have to do."

Emmy nodded. "Okay. Let's go."

We skated toward the party room. I let Emmy tell Kylie all her other friends had

arrived. We helped them bring the presents into the party room, then invited everyone to skate.

I stood by Mom as they all rushed out to skate. It was okay if they skated without me. The important thing was that

Kylie got to hang out with her friends.

A few seconds later, though, Kylie stuck her head back in the room.

"Aren't you coming?" she asked.

I looked at Mom. She nodded, and I skated as fast as I could to catch up. Emmy was waiting outside too. Together, the three of us skated toward the rink, holding hands.

Confetti Fact #9

Did you know you could have your birthday party in all kinds of places? Roller-skating rinks are great, especially if they have party rooms. Here are some other places that might have party rooms:

#1 FAMILY FUN CENTERS

#2 ZOOS

#3 MOVIE THEATERS

#4 BOWLING ALLEYS

#5 TRAMPOLINE SPORTS PLACES

#6 BEAR-BUILDING SHOPS

#7 AQUARIUMS

#8 RESTAURANTS

CHAPTER *10*

"That was a success," Mom said as we pulled out of the parking lot. "Any party where you have a request to help plan another party is a success."

"Then we've had *two* successes!" I said with a ginormous smile. "Both times, someone asked us to plan a party."

"That's right," Mom said. "And my boss is going to be excited to hear that."

"Does that mean we can stay?" I asked.

Mom looked at me. "Is that what you want?"

I looked out the window. We were stuck in the middle of a line of cars, waiting at a traffic light. I liked my new friends. Really, I did. It would be nice to go to school with them in the fall and have sleepovers and do all those fun things.

But then I wouldn't get to have new adventures.

"Do you think we could work at a candy shop?" I asked. "Or maybe the North Pole at Christmas! It's probably really cold up there, though."

Mom laughed. "I can't really promise any of that, but it sounds like you want to keep working in new places."

I thought about that for another second, then nodded. "I think I do. I want to

see where we get to go next. Plus, I'm starting to get better at this 'making friends'
thing."

"Friends are good to have," Mom said.
"But it's important to be able to have them
for a long time. Maybe Emmy and Kylie
could be your real best friends."

"Emmy's okay, but I really like Kylie," I
said. "I want to hang out with her more.
Can we do this just a little longer?"

Mom smiled. I knew I'd told her I
wanted a forever home, but it was only
because I wanted a puppy. I wanted a best
friend, too. But the longer we did this, the
more I felt like I was having more fun with
my mom's different jobs. If we still lived at
our old place, I'd just be hanging out with
my friends all summer. I wouldn't have gotten to play with elephants at the circus or

work in a principal's office or plan these fun parties.

"Just a little longer," Mom said. "And then we'll find our home."

Mom reached her hand back toward the backseat. I reached forward and put my little hand in hers. That was like a secret handshake. We had a plan. And a promise.